And There Were in That Same Country

A Christmas Story

Julie-Allyson Ieron

AND THERE WERE IN THAT SAME COUNTRY

© Copyright 2016

JULIE-ALLYSON IERON

Published in Partnership with:

Joy Media
Park Ridge, IL 60068
http://joymediaservices.com

Cover created by: Joy Media
Cover image in the public domain, located on Pixabay.com.

Interior images adapted from those in the public domain found on Pixabay.com, freeimages.com, publicdomainpictures.com, and publicdomain.nypl.org. Select images from Broderbund ClickArt.

Interior created by: Joy Media Productions

A portion of this story first appeared in *The Standard* magazine and *Pearls to Treasure* © 2010, a Joy Media Publication.

ISBN: 978-1-945818-20-2

For Joyce,

The inspiration behind my love for God's Word and passion to understand how the truth of God's story makes a difference in life today and tomorrow and always.

I love you, Mom!

Contents

Once upon a time, a time not awfully different from today, in a land not very far away, there lived a good king—a perfectly good king.

From his tower high above the land the king looked down to survey his dominion.

F irst, he focused on his capital city. His eyes swept over the dusty cityscape. He saw the place his father used to live. He saw a man who worked in his father's house.

This place and this man made him sad. Not for the first time, nor the last. And this is what he saw.

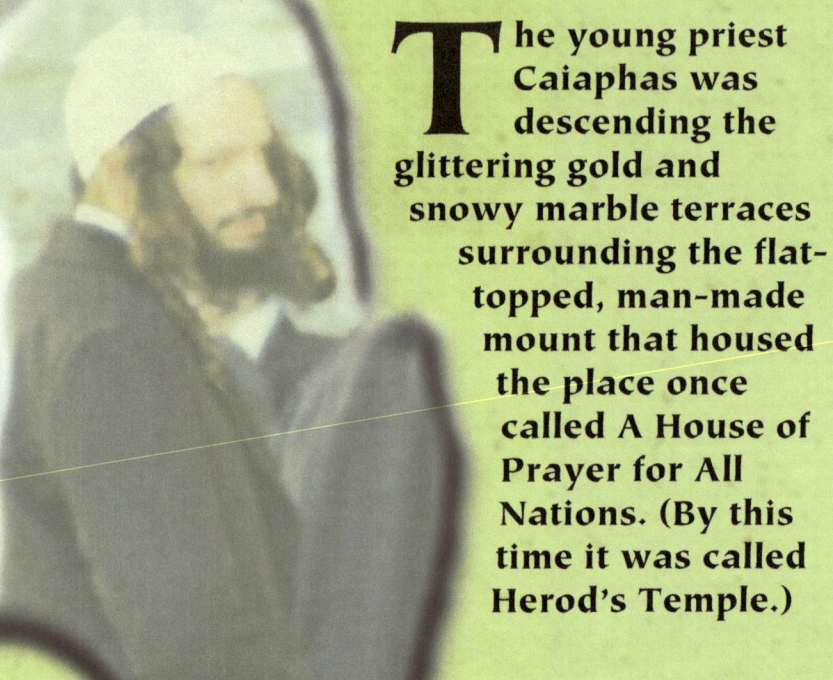

The young priest Caiaphas was descending the glittering gold and snowy marble terraces surrounding the flat-topped, man-made mount that housed the place once called A House of Prayer for All Nations. (By this time it was called Herod's Temple.)

Caiaphas whistled heartily as he passed the raucous barkers calling out to foreigners to exchange their money for temple money—for a small fee, of course.

As he walked down the dusty brown street that led outside the city gate past the place of the skull, a phrase his teacher had used years ago reverberated in his mind. Caiaphas had watched his first sacrifice—heard that pure

lamb bleat, looked on
as it bled, smelled its flesh
as it burned.

His teacher had said it was
necessary for one lamb to die
so the people wouldn't have to.
That made him shudder—then and now.

But he would have none of those haunting
thoughts today. Today he was on a
mission. No longer a student, Caiaphas now
could focus his efforts on buying the hand of the
silly-headed daughter of Annas. She was certain
to cost him plenty. Actually, he cared little for the
girl, scarcely knew her name. It was Annas he
sought out.

Annas controlled the high
priesthood. And that was what Caiaphas wanted
to be. High priest. With all its pomp
and circumstance, power and
influence. And its wealth. Definitely
its wealth. Yes, he would have the
daughter of Annas for his wife.

And he would have the high
priesthood, just you wait and
see.

The good king peered into the young man's heart until he could stand it no longer.

Try as he might to find a spark of love or true wisdom, he found none.

He would have to use this Caiaphas in his grand plan, but the king wished it were not so. The people desperately needed a good high priest—a truly good one.

And that's who they would have. Soon. As soon as the time was right.

Whilst he looked away from the young man, the king saw an elder passing by on the street.

"What about him?" the king mused.

A scroll under his arm, the elder—Nicodemus—moved swiftly, his robes swishing up a cloud of dust in his wake. He had been studying the nuances of the historic law, as it regarded the carrying of a needle in one's robe on the Sabbath day, and he was prepared to report his research results to the seventy men who sat with him on the highest council.

Passing the city's judgment gate (that led to the hill where guilty men were left to die on rough-hewn crosses), and through the shadows of the massive stone walls and pillars that dated back so many generations, he remembered a passage he had read from the scroll in the synagogue just last Sabbath: "Lift up your heads, oh you gates; be lifted up, you ancient doors, that the King of glory may come in. Who is this King of glory? The Lord strong and mighty, the Lord mighty in battle."

Nicodemus found himself wondering, "Who *is* He, this King of glory?"

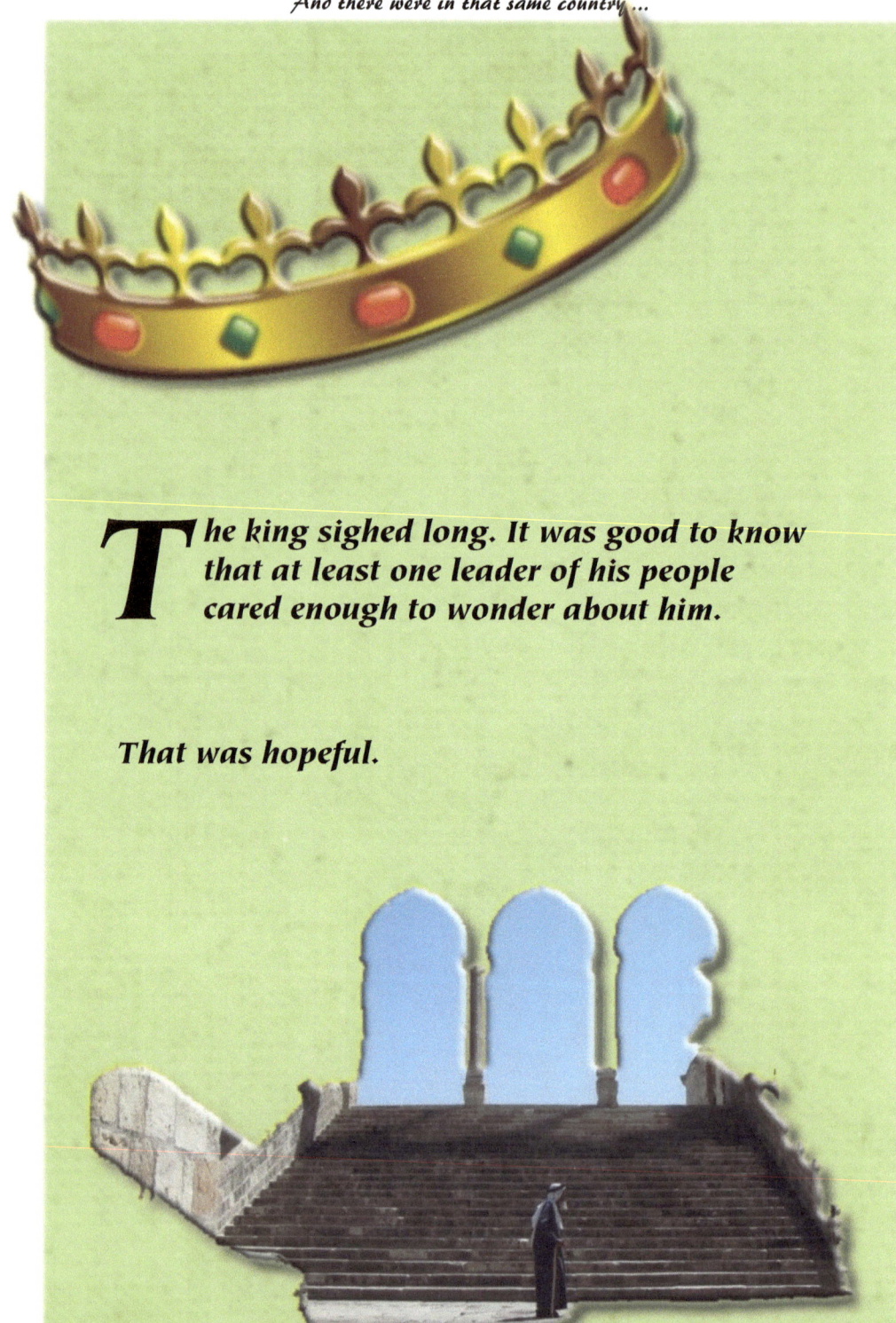

The king sighed long. It was good to know that at least one leader of his people cared enough to wonder about him.

That was hopeful.

Reassured, the king turned his attention to a well two miles to the south and east of the city, a well where the girls of the village of Bethany were gathering to draw the morning water.

It was still cool, the sun barely up, when the little girl Mary left her sister Martha and her baby brother Lazarus at home and skipped off (as well as a little girl can with a clay jug on her head) to draw her family's daily allotment of water.

The other girls her age stood chattering and giggling as they balanced their water jars to minimize the inevitable splashing.

By the time Mary approached, the girls had begun whispering about the hunched-up elderly woman, clay jug painfully clutched, who was approaching the well. Quickly, with many pointed fingers and sideways glances, the girls finished their work and dispersed.

Mary looked up from drawing her water and smiled. She asked whether the woman would like her to fill the jug. The woman nodded her thanks and handed the vessel to the little girl. It was almost as big as the child. But Mary handled it expertly.

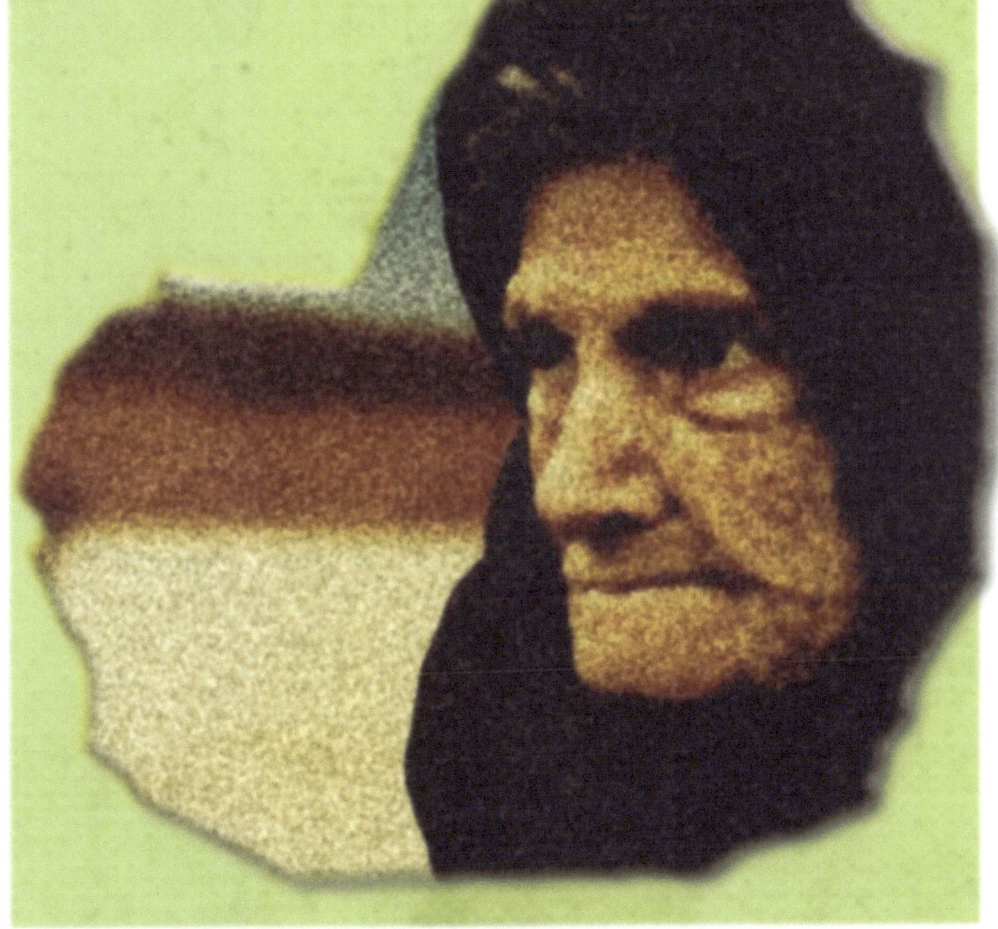

For years the old woman had carried with her a vial of wonderful-smelling spikenard. Though the vial was sealed, the ointment's magnificent aroma strayed through its walls. She had saved it for some noble purpose, not knowing what.

Seeing Mary, she felt compelled to give it to this child. Perhaps it was the reflection in Mary of her own daughter, who had been taken from her many years before. Impulsive, but a good-hearted child.

Perhaps it was—well, no matter. Reaching into her garments, the woman slowly removed the tiny, rose-purple cylinder.

Maybe Mary would find a grand use for the fragrant ointment some day after the woman was long gone.

So, she pressed it into the girl's hand.

Startled by the gift, little Mary hugged her and ran off—forgetting her own water jar.

The king watched as Mary buried the treasure in a secret hiding place, and he knew one day that vial of nard would certainly serve a noble purpose.

But what of the world that didn't yet acknowledge his father's right to rule? The king didn't have to look far to find representatives of the empire that was taxing and tormenting his people.

H e located a battalion of soldiers stationed a few paces from his father's house of prayer. Among that crowd one young man stood out.

Cornelius surveyed his surroundings as he set his club on the dusty ground and brushed off his red wool tunic. This was the second posting since his promotion from legionary to cohort in the army. If he kept at his work with seriousness and refrained from the pillaging and harassing done by his fellow soldiers, in a matter of years he'd be elevated to centurion.

He loved the white cloaks and plumes of the centurion. Helmets adorned with ornate crests. Chest plates ornamented with medals.

His first posting had been uneventful. Ordinary in culture, from top to bottom and back again. But this posting was different.

This group of subjects had its own God, only one. How odd in contrast to the many gods celebrated by his people.

Cornelius shoved himself away from the loud-mouthed battalion, and tuned his ear toward the mournful call of the ram's horn. The sweet sound of song echoed down the steps of the temple; he picked out the words one at a time. Something about them rang clearly in his ear.

"Adonai Eloheinu Adonai echad." He'd been studying their language. He translated it in his mind:

> The Lord our God, the Lord is One.
> Blessed be the Name of His glorious
> kingdom for ever and ever.

And you shall love the Lord your God with all your heart and with all your soul and with all your might.

And these words that I command you today shall be in your heart.

There was something alluring about this one God. He demanded respect and honor, certainly, but expressed love toward His people.

And, as he listened on, Cornelius heard that this God promised rain for the land, grain and oil and cattle and every good thing needed for living.

One God? With such clear and reasonable expectations? He hoped he'd stay here long enough to find out if this could be true.

The king considered this man, unique among his cohorts. He would make a point of encountering this soldier, Cornelius again.

But now a breath of sea air, was what the king needed. So, he turned toward the northwestern corner of the crystal Sea of Galilee. At the waterfront of Capernaum, he watched two fishermen—one expert and elder, the other young and fumbling.

"**Z**ebedee, where is your mind today, man? Watch what you're doing! You're going to tear a net and then what are you going to use to support your new wife and the children you'll have one day?"

"Aw, Dad, you know I'm just anxious to go sign the agreement with my future father-in-law. I want to get on with it! I want to live! I want to start a good life with my fair Salome."

"There'll be time for that, my boy!" Johannas whapped his son on the back of the head. "Now there are lessons to be learned here."

Lessons there were. Cleaning massive nets. Mending tears in their woven mesh. Drying them properly so they wouldn't rot. Weaving fresh stone weights into just the right places.

It was a decent living. Honorable, if smelly work. Most nights shoals of fish were plentiful enough. Especially when they cast a net from their boat across to the boat owned by the Simon family.

When they dragged the net together, using their strong sons to do the heavy lifting, they hauled in catches sufficient to support their families and even a few servants.

Zebedee was re-energized, now, to pay attention, work quickly, and make it back to the house in time.

Just then Zeb's grandfather, Jamus, hobbled down to the boat. Amusement registered on his face, as if he'd just heard the punch line of a favorite joke.

Jamus slapped his son on the back. "John-boy, I remember you as an impetuous young man who tangled every net he touched until I let him go pledge his troth.

"Let young Zeb go. I'll work these nets with you. It hasn't been so long that these gnarled fingers don't remember how."

The king smiled as he watched this thunderous family of fishermen.

Tough. Skilled. Impetuous. Loving. Good stock, who served his father well.

Into the future, he could see two sons Salome and Zebedee would raise, in the same tradition as the family had for generations. The king nodded; this is as it should be.

Then the good king turned his attention to a hillside where young people—mere children—were learning to tend a flock of sheep.

He watched as the children listened intently, and a bit fearfully while their father spoke of the dangers hiding in the falling shadows. Dangers to the lambs and dangers to the children. He spoke of the shepherd's responsibility to lay down his or her life to protect the flock. The children nodded, as they promised to be good shepherds.

It was a weighty job, as this particular flock was specially bred for use in his father's city, a six-mile journey from their grazing land outside the tiny village of Bethlehem. In fact, these lambs were destined for his father's temple.

It was nearly nightfall when the two children coaxed and cajoled the sheep into a makeshift pen that they and their father had constructed. The pen sat tall amid the scruffy, sandy landscape where they had found sufficient tufts of green to nourish the flock. They had painstakingly dragged each of the boulders into position to create a perimeter that would discourage predatory animals whose domain was the impending darkness.

Marcus rattled off the name of each new lamb as his sister shepherded them past the gate. Occasionally he'd poke her with the end of his crook. "Be careful of that one, Little Anna. it's a first-born male. That one is destined to go to the temple for sacrifice."

Her response never changed. "Why does that one have to die, Marcus? He's so little and sweet. He's a beautiful lamb. His wool would make our mama a magnificent shawl. Why do we have to send *this* lamb?"

"Only the best are worthy of our good king, Anna. Dad has told you that every time you wanted to spare a lamb from its destiny."

The little girl didn't seem satisfied, but she continued her herding.

Once all were safely in the enclosure, Marcus (who would celebrate his twelfth year in just a month) plopped himself on the ground, using his body to block the exit of any lamb who might get the idea to wander away before morning light.

Anna looked toward the sunset and her lip began to quiver. "It's awfully dark out here. Not many stars tonight." It was, after all, her first night watching the sheep with just her brother. It wasn't bad, you see, when her daddy was guarding the sheep gate. But her brother was her teaser, her sometimes-tormenter (as all brothers are when it comes to little sisters). Could she trust him?

Marcus sat up straight and tall. "Don't worry Little Anna. *I'll* protect you."

The king recognized the boy's swagger. Trying to be a man, but still a child at heart. The king also knew how little it would take to shatter the boy's bravado.

Then he gazed up the shallow hill, where the family's compound lay. Yes, as he knew would be the case, the children's daddy was standing, watching—out of sight to them, but within range to hear and spring into action if their screams (or any other unnatural event) were to pierce the night.

But for now he had seen enough. Enough to know now was the time he needed to visit his people.

Walk with them.

Eat with them.

Tell stories and laugh with them.

Put his hand on their shoulders and raise up those who felt sad.

Protect them from dangers, and heal them when they hurt.

Now was the time. And he knew—as all kings do—that you can't do that when you look like a king.

So he found a home comfortable and snug in the womb of another young girl, also called Mary, who was newly pledged to a good man—a carpenter.

W hile this Mary and her new husband were visiting his native city of Bethlehem (so they could be counted for the governor's taxation), the king decided to take his first breath of his country's air.

The family home was bulging with relatives, the eldest of whom were staying in the guest chamber.

In the culture of that day, the eldest were due the greatest honor and respect. So, it was expected, even natural, that they would enjoy the hospitality of the family's best chamber.

Of course, no one realized where the king was hiding, or that he was about to make his momentous entrance. Then again, no one expected a king to come dressed in the skin of an ordinary, peasant baby.

So, the only quiet place found for the king (in disguise) to be born was in the cave stable on the house's first floor.

It was the place where the livestock were warmed and fed during the cold season. It was part of the house—technically, but it was somehow more peaceful than the chaotic main chamber, bustling as it was with visitors and distant relatives from across his land.

And so it was that the king cried his first infant cry and made his royal entrance.

His castle traded for a cave stable.

His servants traded for a teenage mother and her carpenter husband.

His throne and ornately majestic dais traded for a cattle trough lined with straw.

His throngs of angelic worshippers traded for a family of shepherd children, their bleating flock of temple sheep, and their watchful father.

And his mother named him Jesus.

So the king came to his own people, but most of them did not receive him.

Still, to all those who did receive him, the ones who believed in his name, he gave the right to become children of God.

—adapted from John 1:11–12

Questions
for further consideration

Have you ever stopped to wonder what else was going on in the world on the night when an angel choir lit up the sky and announced the birth of the world's Savior?

- What were the key players in the Easter story doing on that first Christmas Eve?

- How ordinary was their life in those hours?

- Did they even know or recognize the King when He made His entrance?

- What was God thinking when He chose to send His Son to earth in this way?

This is a rich area of study, worthy of serious discussion and consideration during the Christmas season—and all year long. Here are a few questions to stir your thoughts and direct your conversation with family and friends.

1. What do you suppose Jesus would see if He were to come down and survey your everyday world? What would stand out to Him? What would please Him? What would disappoint Him?

2. How was God preparing each person in the story you just read? What choices did the individuals have? Which of them made good choices? Which made bad choices? How do you know?

3. What traditions do your family members pass down from generation to generation? Why is it important to appreciate and pass along your heritage? What new traditions would you like to introduce?

4. What was it about the prayer the Cornelius character heard that attracted him to the faith? In the story of Jesus' crucifixion a centurion makes the bold claim that Jesus must have been the Son of God. In Acts 10, a Roman centurion named Cornelius was called into God's kingdom because he was seeking to learn more about the God of Israel. Why is it so exciting that God called to Cornelius and the man chose to believe in Him? Why do you suppose he was open to believing in Jesus while the high priest Caiaphas refused to believe?

5. Why couldn't the King of Glory come to earth and mingle with real people while wearing all His kingly nature openly? Why did He have to be born in a stable instead of a castle? What did He give up to be born into this world He created? (See Philippians 2 for hints.)

6. Try explaining what a sacrifice is and why little lambs needed to be sacrificed to pay for the sins of the people. If you're having trouble understanding it, look up Hebrews 5:1-5 and discuss it. Then move to Hebrews 9:24-26 and talk about the difference between sacrificing Bethlehem lambs on the Temple's altar and Jesus sacrificing Himself once and for all on the Cross of Calvary. Which sacrifice is better? Why? Knowing this, what will you do about it this Christmas?

I f these topics pique your interest, here are a few trustworthy sources that can satisfy your curiosity. In fact, Julie is indebted to the following sources for background she used for these stories:

- The Life and Times of Jesus the Messiah, *Alfred Edersheim; Longmans, Green and Co., New York; 1901.*

- Everyday Life in New Testament Times, *A.C. Bouquet; Charles Scribner's Sons Publishers, New York; 1954.*

- The Oxford Companion to the Bible, *edited by Bruce Metzger and Michael Coogan, Oxford University Press, New York; 1993.*

- Mary's Journal: A Mother's Story, *by Evelyn Bence; Zondervan Publishing House, Grand Rapids, Mich.; 1992.*

- Ray VanderLaan's excellent video series, *That the World May Know*, and its companion materials on the web, including: https://www.thattheworldmayknow.com/they-left-their-nets-behind a marvelous study of fishing and https://www.thattheworldmayknow.com/shepherd-lifestyle a description of shepherding in Bible times.

- Bible.org: https://bible.org/article/roman-military-new-testament on Roman Military of Jesus' time.

www.ingramcontent.com/pod-product-compliance
Lightning Source LLC
Chambersburg PA
CBHW041753180626
46815CB00017B/26